Speedy Bee's Dance

Story by Jenny Giles

Illustrations by Isabel Lowe

D1465945

Rigby®

A Harcourt Achieve Imprint

www.Rigby.com

1-800-531-5015

Speedy Bee came back to the hive
with some food
for the baby bees.

"I went all the way
to the blue flowers
to get this food," she said.

"The baby bees are **very** hungry!"
said Speedy Bee.

"We will go and get
some food, too,"
said the bees in the hive.
"Where are the blue flowers?
Dance for us, Speedy Bee."

"Here is my dance," said Speedy Bee.

"Fly this way,
with the sun on your backs.
Fly this way
to the flowers," she said.

The bees looked at the dance.

"**Fly this way,**
with the sun on your backs.
Fly this way
to the flowers," said Speedy Bee.

Away went the bees.

They went on and on and on.

"Look!" said the bees.

"Here are the blue flowers!"

They went flying down
to the flowers.

The bees came back to the hive.

"Speedy Bee's dance
helped us find the blue flowers,"
they said.

"And we **all** got some food

for the hungry baby bees."